Consultant: Gussie Hearsey
On behalf of the Pre-school Playgroups Association

First published 1987 in Germany by Loewes Verlag as
Kein Pudding für Ausreißer

This edition first published 1988 in the United
States by Ideals Publishing Corporation
Nelson Place at Elm Hill Pike
Nashville, TN 37214
Originally published 1988 in Great Britain by
Walker Books Ltd., London

Text © 1987 Norbert Landa
Illustrations © 1987 and 1988 Hanne Türk
English translation © 1988 Patricia Crampton

Printed and bound in Italy by L.E.G.O., Vicenza

ISBN 0-8249-8298-3

BRUIN

No Treats in the Tree House

Written by
Norbert Landa

Illustrated by
Hanne Türk

Translated by
Patricia Crampton

Ideals Publishing Corp.
Nashville, Tennessee

"Here's a treat for the pair of you,"
said Grandpa Bruin. "And today we're going to
be fair. Bruin can cut the treat."

"Oh yes!" cried Bruin,
and he cut the treat.

"And now Susie Bruin can choose
which helping she wants,"
said Grandpa Bruin, chuckling.

"Oh no!" cried Bruin. "The biggest helping
is for me. Because I'm the biggest,
and a treat tastes twice as good to me!"

"If you love me," Bruin sobbed,
"you must be nice to me,
or I'll pack my things
and run away!"
"No treats *there*,"
Susie Bruin murmured.
And there was no big helping
left for Bruin, either.

So Bruin packed up his important things,
all the things a real runaway needs.
Transistor radio.
Football.
Floppy doll.
Cuddly blanket.
Watercolor paints.
Woolly hat.
And dessertspoon.
But it was much too heavy. So only
the most important things could go:
cuddly blanket and dessertspoon –
and a quick cheese sandwich
from the kitchen.

6

Then Bruin set off. He went in a
very, very large circle around the
Bruin house – around the back to the
tree house.
This is a good place for a runaway,
he thought. This is where I'll
stay, all on my very own.

When he was hungry, he ate the
cheese. And when he was still
hungry, he ate the bread as well.

"Look, runaway, I've brought you sandwiches for supper," said Susie Bruin.
"I don't want any sandwiches!" cried Bruin.
"All I want is my treat!"

"Do you want a warm blanket?"
asked Grandpa Bruin.
"You might catch cold,
out here in the night."

"All right," said Bruin,
"but I can tuck myself in."

Then, in the darkness of the night,
Bruin heard a toad – *quarr, quarr!*
I'm not afraid of ghosts,
or snakes, or any old cold
wet toads, thought Bruin.
They can't climb trees.
Quarr, quarr!

Is it really true that toads
can't climb trees – and leap on
lonely little Bruins from behind?

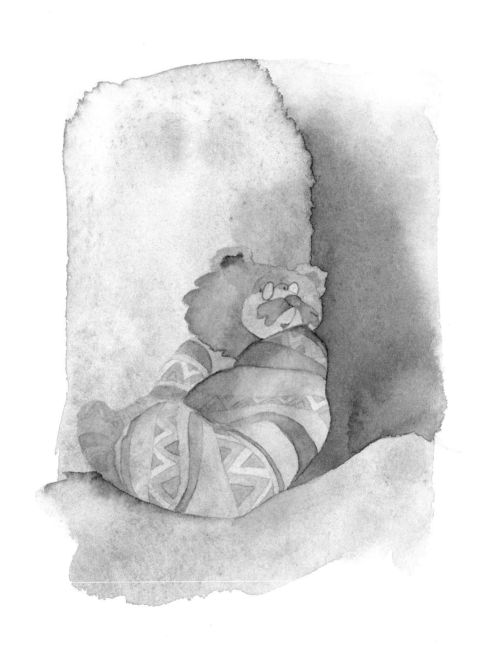

"Help!" Bruin cried.

And then someone else said,
"Shoo, toads, go home! Little Bruins
can easily get frightened in the dark!"

Bruin sighed with relief. It's Grandpa Bruin,
he thought, he's taking care of me. He's
keeping watch and chasing away toads
and anything else that frightens me.
Bruin could go to sleep at last.

In the morning he woke up and thought of
Grandpa Bruin and Susie Bruin and Fred Parrot.
And what he thought made him sad.
He climbed down and set off on the long
road home.

"Going home is a hundred times harder
than running away," sighed Bruin.
"And it would be a hundred times nicer,
if only I could take something back!"
Luckily Bruin found a lot of
sweet blackberries and put them all,
yes, really, *all* of them in his handkerchief
and did not eat a single one.

"It's me," mumbled Bruin, "and good morning and I've brought something home for you."

So then there were blackberry pancakes
for Susie Bruin and Bruin.
And who ate the biggest helping?
Neither of them, because they both
ate just as much as each other,
because they were both feeling just as hungry,
and afterward they both had
just the same fat, round tummies.